THE CHERRY SUNDAE COMPANY

Isla Dewar

LARGE
PRINT

QUICK & EASY

First published in 2004 by
Sandstone Press
This Large Print edition published
2007 by BBC Audiobooks
by arrangement with
Sandstone Press Ltd

ISBN 978 1 405 62223 3

British Library Cataloguing in Publication Data available

Printed and bound in Great Britain by
Antony Rowe Ltd., Chippenham, Wiltshire

WHALES

It started with whales. I saw them on the telly swimming deep in the ocean, calling to one another, whale songs that rang out for miles and miles under the waves. I thought them wonderful. I remember talking about them all the time, boring my mother and father, probably.

When I discovered how whales were being slaughtered for their blubber and meat, and that some species were nearly wiped out, I was furious. I went on and on about it. I cried. I refused to eat, even pizza which was my favourite at the time. I made posters which I put up in the bar of my parents' hotel, the 'Stag and Thistle'. I gave a talk on saving the whale to my class at school. I held a protest march up and down

1

the village square, carrying a placard I'd made myself.

I marched alone. The latest Indiana Jones film was showing in Inverness that day. But I can't say it wasn't fruitful. I came home with two apples, a Twix, fifty pence and a couple of fairy cakes. I put the money in the Save The Whale collection box I'd set up on the bar. It raised £25.14p which I sent to Greenpeace. I was eight at the time.

But that was the start of it. After that I campaigned for tigers, dolphins, pandas and then for children dying of AIDS in Africa, and orphans in Romania. Oh, all sorts of things. Whenever I heard of some injustice, I got angry. Seal culls, motorways cutting through wonderful landscapes, ancient trees cut down, people starving, wars, famine, disease. There was always a lot to feed my fury.

And I wasn't always alone. In time Tina joined my protests. She arrived in the village a year after my Save The Whale march. On her first day at school our teacher, Miss Matheson, put her in the desk next to mine. I told her I was Katy Jameson and did she like Scooby Doo? She said she was Tina Adams and Scooby Doo was her favourite. We agreed that while strawberry ice cream was good, it wasn't as good as chocolate. We both preferred red pencils to blue, especially if they had a rubber on the end. We both wanted a Harley Davidson motorbike for Christmas, but had a feeling we weren't going to get one. We both liked the Birdy Song, though neither of our mums or dads did. In fact, they hated it. We had a really bonding ten minutes of chat before Miss Matheson told us to stop talking and get on with our multiplication sums.

At break time I quizzed Tina, did she like whales? Did she know they were being killed so their fat could be used in soap and make-up? She told me whales were her favourite animals along with dolphins and tigers, and she didn't know they were being killed so people could have soap and make-up. She promised she would never wash her face again as long as she lived, who needed soap?

That was that. I told her she could be my best friend. And best friends we have been ever since that morning sixteen years ago.

Our lives were entwined. We discovered life, lipstick, boys, music, dancing and sex (though not necessarily in that order) together. Through all that growing up we continued our crusades. We did silly stunts for Children In Need, nagged our parents to sponsor kids in the third world, wrote to anybody we could think of to help save animals threatened with extinction. The box on the bar at the hotel that had once said Save The Whale on the side had been replaced by a plain blue tin that said Katy's Campaigns.

That tin raised about fifty pounds a month—people dropping in some change after buying a drink, mostly. Nobody ever questioned where the money went to, it was just left to me to pick some good cause.

I think we did some good. But there was one thing that bothered us all our young lives, and we never did manage to do anything about it. Rodger Barnes Chickens, or rather, Rodger Barnes Battery Hens.

When we were about thirteen Tina and I had seen a documentary about the way battery chickens are reared. It inflamed rage in us both. The cruel conditions, chickens being overcrowded, having their beaks clipped so they couldn't peck one another, the horrible way they were killed, plucked and packed ready to be shipped out to supermarkets It was all horrible.

Rodger Barnes owns a battery hen operation on the edge of our village.

We mounted a campaign against him. At least twice a month, we'd go and stand at the gates of his factory waving banners that said, BAN BATTERY CHICKENS and PLUCK RODGER BARNES. It did no good. Rodger would wave to us as he swished past in his Bentley. Often he would drive through a puddle and spray us with muddy water. Every time we saw him in the village, or coming out of his factory, we'd boo and hiss.

Nobody supported us in this campaign. Rodger Barnes employed far too many people locally for anybody to make trouble. Every family had at least one member who worked for him. Over the years, Rodger has started employing immigrants, but they work longer hours than locals, and for a lot less money.

Time passed, and the battery chicken operation went from strength to strength. Rodger Barnes got richer and richer. And Tina and I grew up. I went to catering college. Tina took a year out after school to go travelling in Australia, then she did four years at Glasgow School of Art.

Now she's back in the village, but planning to move on again. She's thinking of going back to Glasgow to work in art therapy. She wants me to go with her. 'There's plenty work in catering,' she says.

I might go. I haven't made up my mind, yet. I don't know. That's how I am with big life decisions. I can never make them, I just don't know.

THE VILLAGE

Langburgh has grown since I was little. New housing schemes spread out on all sides, but the centre is still the same. If you were a stranger here, it'd take you five minutes to walk down the High Street. But if you're local, it could take over an hour. You'd always meet several people you knew and would have to stop and chat. It's that sort of place.

The centre of the village is a square, in the middle of that is a war memorial. That's where me and my mates used to gather when we were kids. The hotel is on one side of the street, the town hall on the other. There are a few shops, a butcher's, a jeweller's, May Bunting the florist, and Jack Hanley's grocer's shop. Jack's isn't as busy as it once was now that there's a Sainsbury's on the outskirts near the small industrial estate.

Mostly, everybody knows everybody. But the new housing schemes have brought in a lot of new faces. As our hotel is the only drinking hole, all the incomers have been pretty good for business. I came back to work here straight out of college, so I have only spent a year away from home. Some of my friends, though, never left at all. They were born here, got married here, are raising their own kids here and no doubt, one day they'll die here. Others left and never came back.

There's lots to do. Everything that happens mostly takes place at the town hall. Mondays there's the weight watchers, Tuesdays the W.R.I., Wednesdays the dramatic society. I joined that a couple of years ago. I'm the prompt. I have no desire to leap about on stage. We mostly do musicals. This year it's South Pacific. Anyway, on Thursdays there's a book group in the small room upstairs and Bingo in the main hall. Fridays is youth club night, always has been.

We have other things going on. There's the bowling club, the tennis club, the gardeners' club, the chess club (very small, they meet in the Simon Jackson's living room, there's only three members) and, naturally, the golf club, president Rodger Barnes. I am never going to join the golf club. We also have various societies that meet in the back room of the hotel—the art society, the history society, the madrigal society and a poetry society.

You could say Langburgh was a humming place. But I remember being fifteen, and thinking there was absolutely nothing to do. I don't really blame people for leaving, looking for big city life.

Still, all these clubs are also good

for business, since when their meetings end they all end up in the bar of the Stag and Thistle.

The night the whole stupid Cherry Sundae Company thing started was when the weight watchers were in talking calories and crowing about how much they'd lost, or moaning about how much they hadn't lost. So it must have been a Monday.

Vera Sanders, who is painfully thin, had come up to the bar and ordered her usual sherry. I have no idea why Vera is a member of weight watchers. She has no flesh on her at all, sometimes you think that if she bent down quickly—say, to pick up a fiver she'd dropped—she might snap in two. I think she just goes along Monday nights for the company. She lives on Bramwell Road in the house she shared with her mother before she died about six years ago.

She has an air of sadness about her, Vera. I've always thought it's because she lives in the dark. Her next door neighbour has let his hedge grow so it's over fifteen feet high. It stops any light getting into her house or garden. She has to have her lights on all day, and I suppose her electricity bill must be enormous. Everyone knows she has very little money. She's over sixty, and worked all her life in the accounts department of the chicken farm. She retired a few years ago with no pension. I think they gave her a watch as a retirement present. I don't know though. If they did, she mustn't like it, she never wears it.

She is a member of the gardeners' club, but doesn't often go along to the meetings. She says it depresses her. All the flowers people talk about, and her garden gets no sun, she can only grow deep shade plants. 'I sigh for delphiniums and poppies,' she told me, once.

That night, Tina was at the bar drinking a vodka and tonic. I was serving and drinking coffee, because

I don't take alcohol when I'm working. Vera tapped a pound coin on the counter and asked for her usual, sherry. I filled a glass, put it in front of her and took the money. 'That's fifty pence, Vera.' I gave her two twenty pences and a ten in change.

I do this because she always puts something in the campaign box, and if I gave her a fifty pence piece back, she'd put that in. Well, this is a woman on a tight budget. Her Monday nights are carefully costed out. Fifty pence for a drink, twenty for the box on the bar.

'Fifty pence? For a sherry?' Tina said when Vera had taken her drink over to the seat by the fire. 'I think I'll change drinks.'

'Only Vera gets sherry for fifty pence,' I said. 'Everyone else has to pay the full price.'

'So why is she so honoured?' asked Tina.

'She hasn't much money. If she

paid full price, she probably wouldn't come for a drink and she enjoys the company and the warmth,' I said. And I explained about Vera living alone, and about the massive hedge that shut out all her light. 'She must have huge heating and lighting bills. Her house gets damp because no sun gets to it. It's depressing.'

Tina said, 'Why doesn't she make her neighbour cut down his hedge?'

'It's on his ground. He just refuses to cut it down.'

'There should be a law,' Tina said.

I said that I thought there might be one, but if there was her neighbour didn't care about it.

'Well, you should cut down the hedge,' said Tina.

'Me?'

'Why not? You're always banging on about the unfairness of things. You're always sending money off to distant parts of the world to help people in distress. What about folks here under your nose?' She banged

15

her fist on the bar. 'Charity begins at home, y'know.'

I thought about that. She was right, of course. If I'd heard about people in Africa or India whose lives were made miserable because of hedges blocking their light, I'd have marched in protest, I'd have raised money, I'd have shouted and screamed about it. It never crossed my mind that I should do something to help Vera. But what was happening to her was wrong. And if nobody else was going to do something, then it was up to me.

'OK,' I said. 'I will. I'll cut down that hedge. And you can help.'

That was the start of it.

THE CHERRY SUNDAE COMPANY

Cutting down someone's hedge isn't easy. Especially when that someone plainly does not want their hedge cut down. It took some planning.

The next week, when Vera came in for a sherry I asked her why she didn't cut down the hedge herself.

'Well,' she said. 'It's too high. I haven't got a ladder. And even if I did, I wouldn't go up it. I hate heights. Besides, I'd have to do it on a Tuesday. That's the only time Mr Baker is away.'

Mr Baker (Vera didn't know his first name), worked from home—something to do with computers. But on Tuesdays he went to Glasgow to his head office for a weekly meeting. He usually got home sometime after eight o'clock in the evening.

'But on Tuesdays, I go to Inverness to meet my sister for lunch, and have a bit of a look round the shops. So I couldn't do it then, even if I could do it at all, which I couldn't.'

I said, 'Ah, right.' And thought, Tuesday it will be, then.

Our real problem was transport. My dad has a cordless hedge trimmer, shears and a ladder in the outhouse at the back of the hotel. I didn't think he'd notice them missing. He's very fond of his power tools. But it's more to do with having them, going out to buy them, rather than actually using them. So we had the stuff to cut the hedge, but no way of getting that stuff to the hedge.

I drive a Mini. There was no way I was going to tie a ladder to its roof. I love that car. Besides, everyone in the village knows it's mine. People would see it parked outside Mr Baker's house, and know it was me doing the dirty to the hedge.

Tina thought we could use Peter's van. Peter is her boyfriend of sorts. They were an item when they were at school and split up when Tina left. They got together again when she came back, but more in a friendly way than before. Now they are chums, well, chums with sex. Which seems like an excellent relationship to me.

Trouble was, Peter is well known about these parts. He's the local painter and decorator. The only thing that's better known than him is his van. It's an eye-dazzling pink, with Peter the Painter on the side in large dark blue letters. You can't miss it.

'We'll have to disguise it,' Tina said.

'How do you disguise a bright pink van?' I said.

'Not easily,' said Tina. 'But it must be possible.'

I said that I'd leave it to her. After all, I was supplying the trimmer, the shears, the ladder and the black bags to put all the clippings in. It was her turn to do something.

A couple of days later she dropped into the hotel. I was in the kitchen preparing the little chocolate puddings for the evening menu. She took one. I slapped her wrist.

'These meals are carefully costed out,' I said. 'I do twenty this time of year. Sixty in the high season. Now there's only nineteen.'

Ignoring me, she asked, 'What would be a good name for our company?'

'What company? We don't have a company.'

'I know that. But it's the name to go on the side of the van.'

'You're never going to spray Peter's van,' I was shocked.

'No. I'm going to spray the sheets of cardboard I'll put over the sides of the van.'

'Won't that be enough?' I said.

'No. It won't. It'll look like a van

with cardboard sides. I'll do the cardboard with metallic paint, then put on a company logo so it looks official. I need a name for the company we are going to pretend to be.'

'The Chocolate Pot Company,' I said.

Tina shook her head. 'Nah, sounds like we did catering.'

'The British Knicker Elastic Company,' I said.

Tina told me not to be silly. But that didn't stop me. I'm naturally silly. 'The Old Underpants Company. The Useless Elbow Company. The Limp . . .'

'Stop,' said Tina. 'You're about to give up being silly and go on to being rude.'

I shrugged. She took out her new lipstick. 'Got it today,' she said rolling it up. It was red and glossy. She likes her lips glowing red. I prefer a more natural pale browny shade.

'Cherry Sundae,' she said.

'Lovely,' I said. 'Then that's what we should call ourselves. The Cherry Sundae Company. It's bright. Sort of tasty and means nothing.'

Tina agreed. And went off to paint it on to the cardboard sheets that would disguise Peter's van.

And that's how we became the Cherry Sundae Company.

TRIMMING THE HEDGE AND OTHER GOOD DEEDS

It's tough trimming a giant hedge. There's more to it than you might think. First thing was the ladder. Neither of us wanted to go up it. It's one thing to say fifteen feet, but being fifteen feet off the ground is a different thing altogether. We tossed for it. I lost.

We were trying not to speak much. We were dressed as blokes, and thought our voices might give us away. I'd borrowed a couple of outfits from the dramatic society's wardrobe. Tina wore a pair of dungarees about three sizes too big and a huge tartan shirt. I wore a blue boiler suit thing. Tina looked better than me. I wished I'd chosen the dungarees. She'd wanted to put on a false moustache, but I thought it might keep slipping off when we were working. What we did do was put on a Groucho Marx mask thing of glasses, nose and huge droopy moustache as we were driving along so nobody would recognise us. We took them off when we pulled up at Vera's neighbour's house. They were so absurd, we couldn't do anything for laughing.

So I climbed the ladder and snipped the top of the hedge with shears while Tina stayed below and gathered the clippings into the black bags we'd brought. We decided to save the electric cutter for the thick branches at the bottom. It only works for an hour before you have to recharge it.

We'd thought the whole thing would take about an hour. It took four. We were hot, sweaty, knackered, filthy. I had bits of hedge down my back, the noise of that cutter drumming in my ears and dust up my nose. Tina, after all that time bent double picking up clippings, couldn't straighten up again.

First we lopped down the hedge on Mr Baker's side, then we went round to Vera's garden and cut it there. We filled over twenty black bags which we packed into the back of the van.

We drove to the municipal dump and dropped the bags into the skip. We took the boards off the van, then dropped it off at Peter's house. And went home.

I had a hot bath. I was aching all over. That was it. The hedge was cut down. It looked short and stubby, but what the hell, the light and sun were flooding Vera's garden. I felt wonderful. Good deed done. I thought that was over. I was wrong.

It was the talk of the village. Not so much the cutting of the hedge, more Mr Baker's reaction to the cutting of the hedge. He accused Vera of doing it. Worse, he'd reported her to the police.

She told me about it next time she came into the bar.

'They questioned me for over an hour,' she said. 'They asked where I'd been on the day. I told them I was with my sister. And they checked up on me. Cheek they have. I feel like a criminal and I haven't done anything.'

I gave her a drink on the house and asked her if she had any idea who'd cut down the hedge.

'Well,' she said. 'Sheila Findlay across the road was watching them.'

Someone was watching us! My stomach churned. I hadn't noticed that.

'And,' Vera went on, 'she says they were an odd looking lot. Two men, quite young and a bit skinny.'

Skinny, I thought. I like that.

'Thing is, Sheila says she was sure they had moustaches when they arrived. Then they didn't have moustaches. Then they did again. Mind you, she's a bit strange that

Sheila. Getting on in years. Past eighty now. I think her mind's going. She says they were in the funniest van. It had Cherry Sundae Company on the side, huge lettering.'

'Cherry Sundae Company,' I said. 'Sounds a bit iffy if you ask me.'

'Definitely,' said Vera. 'One thing, these men knew nothing about gardening. The mess they made of that hedge. It's all scruffy and chopped to bits. And uneven. Sheila Findlay says it looked as if they'd never used a hedge cutter in their lives before. And they were fighting about who was to climb up the ladder.'

That Sheila Findlay's mind is not going, not at all, I thought.

'And now that Baker fellow is threatening to come over and chop down my roses,' said Vera. 'It's all a terrible mess, the whole thing.'

The Cherry Sundae Company is going to have to do something about Mr Baker, I decided and offered

Vera another drink on the house to cheer her up.

Next day I spent time on the computer. I made a letter-heading in bright red, THE CHERRY SUNDAE COMPANY. Below that in smaller letters I wrote 'Watching Over You'.

Then I wrote a letter to Mr Baker.

Dear Mr Baker

The Cherry Sundae Company thanks you for letting light and sun into your neighbour's home. We promote friendliness, and are sending you a reward for your kindness. Please accept this gift of fifty pounds. Remember the Cherry Sundae Company are watching over you, and keeping an eye on your hedge.

Yours in Neighbourliness,
The Cherry Sundae Company.

That'll do it, I thought. Then I had an idea. Why leave it at that? Why not give some money to other people, spread the good word? It might take the heat off Vera.

I sent ten pounds to Janice Spence who works in the chemist because I'd noticed her picking up some litter not long ago.

Dear Janice
The Cherry Sundae Company is sending you this money as a reward for your thoughtful action in removing a crisp bag from the pavement in front of the library last week. Well done. Good deeds will be returned to you many times.

I sent twenty pounds to Mary Hargreaves who is bringing up two kids on her own and sometimes looks a little down.

Dear Mary
The Cherry Sundae Company is sending you this money for

doing a grand job with your kids. They are lovely and it's all down to you. Good deeds will be returned to you many times.

I sent another tenner to George Frazer who always gets library books and shopping for Irene Thompson who lives along the road from him. Irene is housebound.

Dear George
Please accept this small token from the Cherry Sundae Company. Your kindness has not gone unnoticed. Remember good deeds will be returned to you many times.

And I sent another tenner to Charlie Hughes, the postman, who is always smiling and in a good mood.

Dear Charlie
Please find enclosed ten pounds. It is a gift from the

Cherry Sundae Company in recognition of your good humour and with grateful thanks for all the smiling you do. Remember good deeds will be returned to you many times.

I printed out my letters on bright pink paper. Got the money from the charity box in the bar. Put the lot into envelopes. Addressed them. Stamped them. And gave them to Tina to post in Glasgow as she was going there for an interview about an art therapy course.

'That way nobody will think that the Cherry Sundae Company is local,' I said.

'Excellent,' she said.

That's it now, I thought. Sorted.

But I was wrong again. The next day I was working in the kitchen when Jean our lunchtime barmaid came through to get me. 'It's the police,' she said. 'They want to talk to you.'

31

EVERYONE IS BEING GOOD

Have you noticed how policemen can fill a room, even when there's only two of them and the room's quite big? These two blokes in uniform seemed to take up the whole bar. I smiled to them, and picked up a cloth to polish some glasses. I was shaking so much, I needed to do something with my hands.

They wanted to know if I'd seen a couple of men in the bar, one in dungarees, the other in a boiler suit, both skinny and perhaps with moustaches. I shook my head and said I hadn't seen any new faces in the past week.

'It's been quiet,' I said.

They nodded and asked if I'd heard of a Cherry Sundae Company.

I said that some of the customers

had been talking about it, but really it was a new name to me.

There was some truth in this. We'd only thought of the name a few days ago, so in a way it was still new to me.

Rodger Barnes was standing at the bar, drinking a glass of malt whisky. He was watching me, listening to everything that was said.

'Well,' said one of the policemen, 'thanks for your help. We're just following routine inquiries. But if you do see a couple of men answering to our description, please let us know.'

I said I would.

'And,' said his companion, 'if they want to do some gardening work, don't give them any. They know nothing about gardening. The mess they made of that hedge.'

I smiled and told them the garden was my dad's pride and joy. He never let anyone else touch it.

That was when Rodger Barnes

joined in. He said it was a queer old business, a strange company coming along out of the blue and chopping down a hedge.

'I mean,' he said. 'How did they know about that hedge? Must have had some local knowledge.'

The policemen agreed. That's what they thought.

Roger Barnes looked at me, 'You're the do-gooder around here. Wouldn't you have any idea who might be involved?' He turned to the policemen and said, 'She was always protesting about something when she was little. Did a protest march on her own. She collects money to send to starving people across the world. Worries about whales and such like.'

The policemen looked at me. I shrugged.

Then Rodger said, 'Where were you on the day the hedge got clipped, anyway?'

It was like a punch, a left-hook, from nowhere. I really hadn't been expecting that. I think I stood opening and shutting my mouth like a fish. I went red. I couldn't think.

'I can't remember,' I said. Then, 'I went shopping with Tina. It was my day off.' Then I got myself together, 'You think I chopped down the hedge?' And before he could reply, I asked what he'd been doing that day.

'Same as I do every day. I was at work,' he said.

The policemen said they'd leave us to it. But so far they had no suspects. I glared at Rodger. He smirked back. Then I went back to the kitchen. I was making soup of the day, potato and leek. I was so angry I gave the vegetables a serious chopping. That Rodger Barnes, I was thinking, the Cherry Sundae Company are going to have to do something about him.

Over the next few days word spread through the village about the money certain people had received. 'Just for doing a little good,' Vera said. 'It's lovely.'

In fact the word spread so much our local paper heard about it and put a story about it on the front page. THE MYSTERIOUS CHERRY SUNDAE COMPANY, the headline said. Then there were interviews with some of the people who'd got some cash. They all said how amazed they were and how it was so nice that the small things they'd done had been noticed. I was really pleased.

After that I noticed something weird going on. Everyone was going about smiling to one another, big grins. All the time they were looking about, as if they were hoping their huge smiles were being noticed. I saw one or two people picking up litter and making quite a show of walking over to the bin with a sweet wrapper or whatever. It seemed to me that people were acting as if they were being watched. They were hoping the Cherry Sundae Company was spying on them and would send them some money.

Oh well, I supposed that was just the way people were.

Meantime, I was busy plotting and scheming. Rodger Barnes, I thought, the Cherry Sundae Company is after you.

THE BIG STEAL

Things I know about Rodger Barnes:

1. I don't like him.
2. He's a bully.
3. He thinks a lot of himself.
4. He is giving the after dinner speech at the golf club this year.
5. He fancies himself as a collector of art.
6. I don't like him. I mentioned this already. But I really, really don't like him.

He was in the bar not long ago boasting about a picture he'd bought. He'd said it was enormous, full of life and colour. A magnificent piece by someone called Marvin Hay.

Everyone had looked blank.

Nobody had heard of Marvin Hay. But Rodger kept saying how wonderful his work was so we all thought to keep our mouths shut. None of us knew anything about art.

Rodger had gone on to say he'd paid a fortune for the painting, but, hey, what was money when it came to having something beautiful to look at every day.

I can't remember who it was, but someone said, 'C'mon then, Rodger, how much did you pay for the painting?'

Rodger looked a bit sheepish. Then he said, 'Well, actually, thirty grand.'

The bar went quiet. There was a stunned silence. We all let this last remark soak through our brains— thirty grand.

Then Donald McGee said, 'You'll be needing a good security system if you've got something that valuable in your house.'

He would say that, he sells security

systems.

But Rodger said that the painting wasn't in his house, it was in the reception area of his office. 'Who needs security systems round these parts?' he said. 'People don't even lock their door at night.'

Not long after that he'd left. He was thinking, no doubt, that we'd all be impressed. But nobody was, really. People were talking about the hedge getting cut down. That was the subject of the day in the bar.

But, busy in the kitchen after Rodger had asked me what I was doing the day of the great hedge trimming, I got to thinking about that painting. And at some point between taking out my fury on the potatoes and leeks and going to bed that night, I decided I would steal the Rodger Barnes' great work of art.

The golf club annual dinner was on Saturday night. The great robbery would take place then.

I told Tina about it. At first she

wasn't keen. 'Clipping a hedge is one thing. Stealing is something else. We could go to jail.'

'Only if we were caught,' I said. 'And then we'd be first time offenders and would probably get community service. It may be wrong to steal, but it's also wrong to keep chickens in terrible conditions and pay people badly. We'd steal the painting, sell it for a load of money and give the cash to the people who work at the battery hen farm. It'd be like Robin Hood.'

She thought about this, then agreed. 'OK.'

I had it all worked out. Tina would come to the pub on Saturday night. At nine o'clock she'd go to the loo. I'd be working behind the bar, and at the same time I'd tell my Dad I was going to the cellar to get some tonic water as we were running out. I'd get tonic water, leave it behind the back door. Tina would have parked the van at the gate behind the outhouses.

We'd drive out of the village, put on the Cherry Sundae Company boards. Go to Rodger Barnes' factory. Get the painting. Stop on the way back. Take off the boards. Drive to Tina's house. Put the painting in her bedroom under the dustsheet where she keeps all the paintings she did at art school. Leave the van at Peter's house. Run to the pub. Tina would go into the bar as if she was getting back from the loo. I'd go round to the back door and pick up the tonic water and walk back into the bar. It was simple. This time it was my turn to wear the dungarees.

It all went smoothly. It was easy. I'd been in a state of nerves all day. But when the time came to do the job, I was icy. In fact, I was so cool, I thought maybe I was a born thief. The only time we halted in our easy progress was when we saw the picture. It was truly, truly horrible. It was the most hideous painting I had ever seen in my life. There were luminous green blobs on a scarlet background, and along the bottom rows and rows of chickens running, looking alarmed. I hated it.

Tina shone her torch on it and gasped. 'It's revolting.'

I was standing beside her, mouth agape. I was thinking that if I was going to ruin my reputation and become a thief, I'd rather steal something I liked.

'We're not here to question someone's taste,' I said. 'This is an act of charity.'

So we heaved it from the wall—it was very big—and staggered out to the van with it.

The whole thing took about half an hour. I was worried that when I walked back into the bar with the box of tonic water bottles, Dad would ask where I'd been. But he was so busy talking football with a regular, he hadn't noticed me missing.

Tina just slipped back onto her bar

stool and continued drinking the vodka and coke she'd left, and looked like she hadn't even been away.

It took about ten minutes for me to realise what we'd done. I started to shake, and had to go into the kitchen to sit down and get myself together. When I went back into the bar, I poured myself a drink.

Tina watched me. 'Are you all right?' she said.

'No, I'm not,' I said. 'That was too easy. Way, way too easy. Something's wrong.'

THINGS TO CONSIDER

Things to Consider if You Are Going to do a Major Robbery:

1. Make sure the thing you steal is easy to dispose of.
2. It's handy if someone wants to buy the goods from you.
3. Be very suspicious if the place you are robbing is not locked up.
4. If a very valuable thing is easy to steal, perhaps it's not very valuable after all.
5. Make sure the person you steal from is not up to naughtier things than you are.

The robbery was the talk of the village. The hedge was forgotten. It made the headlines in the local paper, and was reported on our local radio station.

The newspaper made interesting reading. Rodger Barnes was very upset about the loss of his beautiful painting. 'It was a work of art and cannot ever be replaced,' he said. Then the article detailed the mess the thieves had made. They had smashed a window when gaining entrance to the building, and had destroyed two other paintings. The security system had been tampered with and disabled.

This was nonsense. The door of the building had been unlocked. We just walked in. We would never smash windows. Rodger Barnes had said he never locked his offices. And there were no other paintings in the reception area. We'd had a good look round. There was only one huge, horrible thing on the far wall facing you as you came in. There had been no security system.

'Weird,' I said to Tina.

'Weird,' she agreed.

'Scary,' I said.

'Weird and scary,' she said.

The article continued, saying the police were investigating the crime and were anxious to speak to anyone who was in the area on the evening the painting was stolen and might have noticed something suspicious.

I felt a grim flutter in my stomach. The sort of feeling you get when you are going to the dentist and know you're going to get a huge filling. Or when you are about to sit an exam and haven't done any studying. I was filled with dread.

The article ended by saying that Rodger Barnes was offering a reward for any information that would lead to the return of the painting.

'Well, what do you make of that?' I said.

'There's something fishy going on,' said Tina. She looked around, checking nobody was listening and lowered her voice to a whisper. 'It says the thieves smashed a window. We didn't do that. And it says two other paintings were damaged. Not true. What's that about?'

'I don't know,' I said.

'Lies. Lies. Lies,' said Tina. 'Why?'

I didn't know.

I could remember everything about that night. Every detail ran through my mind, I could play it over and over in my head like an old and favourite video.

It hadn't been all that dark as we drove out to the chicken farm, but we'd had the van lights on anyway. The beam spread out in front of us, picking up bushes and trees, turning them silvery. We hadn't spoken much, we were both nervous. I remember our breath sounded heavy. The tyres crunched on gravel as we drove up to Rodger Barnes' offices, and after we stopped, we sat for a few minutes. Both of us were scared of what we were about to do. And we were making sure nobody was about. There wasn't a sound, just the wind moving through the trees, and a dog somewhere far off barking.

We were wearing the Groucho masks. And had gloves on, since we didn't want to leave any fingerprints. I tried the window, thinking we'd have to climb in. But as I was doing that, Tina tried the door. It opened. The light from our torch cast shadows as we moved it round the room, over the walls, searching for the picture. We didn't speak. I think we were both holding our breath. Then we saw the picture, and shuddered at the awfulness of it. We lifted it down and carried it out to the van. I went back to the office and closed the front door. I remember I stood for a moment, looking round, listening. There was nobody about. It was silent. I got into the van beside Tina and we drove off.

Now I wondered if perhaps there had been someone standing in the bushes watching us.

We sat in the bar reading the newspaper article. We looked at one another, thinking. The answer came to us both at the same time. 'Insurance,' we said. 'Rodger Barnes is working some sort of insurance scam.'

It didn't take us long to work it out. We decided the painting was worthless. Well, that wasn't hard to figure out. It was hideous. But somehow Rodger had got it insured for thirty thousand pounds. We wondered if he had some sort of block insurance covering all his paintings, and some of them, the ones the insurance company had seen, really were valuable. He'd left the one terrible painting on the wall of his reception area. He'd boasted in public about where it was, how much it was worth and how easy it would be to get hold of. He'd hoped someone would steal it.

He'd known that the thief would be local—you don't get many

international art thieves about these parts. Then with all the publicity the thief wouldn't be able to sell the picture. And even if he or she took it to some gallery to be valued, they'd be a laughing stock, and would be left with a huge and totally horrible painting. Meantime, Rodger had gone to his offices, tampered with his security system, damaged two more paintings and smashed the window to make the robbery look more professional. After all, the insurance company wouldn't give him a penny if they knew he'd left the place unlocked.

We'd been duped. We were the fools left with the monstrosity in Tina's bedroom.

NICE ONE

Tina got accepted for the art therapy course, and I decided to go to Glasgow with her. I didn't need much persuading. I'd lived in the village all my life, and I thought it would do me good to stay in a city for a year or two. I knew I'd come back some day. Small places do that to you. They get under your skin.

Besides, things were getting hot for the Cherry Sundae Company. We had to get rid of the painting. We thought the best thing to do would be to throw it in the local dump late at night before we left. That way it might be discovered, and the person who found it might get the reward. And, we liked this bit, Rodger would get his vile picture back.

I applied for several jobs, all in

catering. Eventually I got accepted by a small restaurant that specialised in organic meals. It suited me well. I'd stayed in Glasgow for a couple of days after my interview and looked for a flat Tina and I could share.

I found one that was within walking distance of Sauchiehall Street. It was quite small, two flights up, one large living room, a tiny kitchen, a bathroom and two bedrooms. Not much of a view, but being near the centre had a real appeal for someone who has always had to travel to the shops or cinema. I wasn't planning to spend much time at home. I had a new life to live.

It was Saturday lunchtime when I got back. The bar was humming, crowded with drinkers. Dad asked me to help, so I dumped my bag in my room and went down to serve.

Rodger Barnes was there. He often drops in for a glass of malt after his game of golf. He was talking about the robbery. In his version the thieves were hard and ruthless.

'People like that wouldn't think twice about shooting you if you caught them in the act,' he said.

'There are some tough nuts around,' said Charlie. He always comes in for a pint on Saturday.

Rodger agreed. 'I haven't much hope of seeing my picture again.'

'What did it look like?' said Charlie.

'Very bright. A wonderful mass of colour. Luminous. And a flock of hens along the bottom. Very meaningful,' said Rodger.

'Right,' said Charlie in a way that showed he didn't think much of what he was hearing.

'It was a true work of art,' said Rodger. 'I'll never see the like again. That's why I'm offering a reward.'

'Yeah,' said Charlie. 'So how much is the reward, anyway?'

'A thousand pounds,' Rodger told him.

I was busy wiping the bar and cleaning glasses. I pretended not to be listening. But I thought a thousand pounds would be quite handy for the person who found the painting in the skip. I wondered if I could write to someone tipping them off about where they might find some treasure.

'A thousand pounds for a man of your means,' said Charlie. 'That's not very much. Surely you could stump up more than that.'

He was joking, of course. Anybody who knows Charlie would know that. He is always teasing people. But Rodger doesn't know Charlie well. And he's far too pompous to know when someone is taking the mickey out of him.

'You think?' he said.

'I know,' said Charlie. And he winked at me.

It worried me, that wink. Did he know? In fact did everyone in the bar know that it was me who took the painting, and that I was the Cherry Sundae Company?

That's another thing about small places. Everyone knows everyone. And everyone knows everyone's business. In fact, sometimes you think people know more about you than you do yourself.

For instance, I was once talking to Vera about my aunt in Australia. I'd said I'd like to go visit her some day. Vera told someone that I was thinking about going to Australia some day. That someone told someone else. Next thing I knew I was going to Australia and had bought a ticket and was leaving the next week. People were coming up to me and telling me how much they'd miss me, but they hoped I'd have a good time and I'd have fun learning to surf on Bondi Beach. It was a bit embarrassing saying that I wasn't going to Inverness never mind the other side of the world.

So that was why the wink bothered

me.

Rodger hadn't seen it. He was thinking about the size of his reward. 'I'll up it to five thousand,' he said.

'Five thousand,' said Charlie trying to sound unimpressed. He shrugged. Now he really was making a fool of Rodger.

The thing about being boastful is you have to keep on boasting. I could see Rodger was irritated that Charlie didn't swoon with amazement at the new sum. He had to keep going till he got the respect and envy he needed. Boasters do that.

'All right,' he said. 'I'll up it. I'll give fifteen thousand pounds to anyone who returns my painting.'

That did it. The bar went quiet. Everyone looked at him.

'Fifteen thousand pounds,' he said. 'No questions asked. Just give me back my picture.'

That did it. He got the reaction he wanted. There was a hush, everyone in the bar stared at him.

Charlie was enjoying himself now. 'You want to put that in writing?' he asked.

'No problem,' said Rodger. He got out his pen. Asked me for some paper. I gave him a sheet of the hotel's headed notepaper.

I, Rodger Barnes, will give fifteen thousand pounds to anyone who returns my painting.

He took the paper over to the notice board beside the fireplace and stuck it up.

'There,' he said. And he looked at Charlie, 'Happy now?'

'Oh yes,' said Charlie and he winked at me again.

For the next two weeks before I left for Glasgow, I thought about the painting and the money. It seemed a pity not to claim fifteen thousand pounds. But how could I do it without being found out as a thief? Besides, the whole point had been to sell the picture and give the money to Rodger's workers.

It took me the two weeks to come up with a solution. It was, if I say so myself, brilliant.

We were due leave on the Sunday morning, and planned to go early. We wanted to get to Glasgow at about mid-day so we could have a look round then get ready for the Monday morning when I was starting my new job and Tina her art therapy course.

Saturday night we packed my Mini. And we took the horrible painting out of Tina's bedroom and put it in the outhouse at the back of the hotel.

At five in the morning, before we left, we took the picture round to the village green and put it on a bench in front of the town hall. Beside it we pinned a note.

Dear Rodger Barnes
Here is your beautiful work of art. The Cherry Sundae Company has found it and is

returning it to you. We are also claiming your fifteen thousand pound reward.

We are asking you to give it to your workers. An equal share for everyone.

Remember your good deeds will be returned to you many times.

With love

The Cherry Sundae Company.

When we'd done that, we went back to the hotel, woke my mum and dad, had breakfast, kissed them goodbye, promised to phone the minute we arrived at our new flat, and left.

We got into town just after one o'clock, and I phoned just after three. We unpacked the van, and carried our stuff up the two flights of stairs to the flat. Decided who was having the front bedroom—Tina. We made a cup of coffee. Then I dialled the hotel. Dad answered.

'How are you?' he asked.

'Fine,' I said. 'The flat's fine. We're settling in.'

'You'll never guess what's happened here,' he said.

'Tell me. Is it good gossip?'

'The best. That painting of Rodger Barnes has turned up outside the town hall. The Cherry Sundae Company, you know, the people who chopped down Vera's hedge, put it there.'

'Never,' I said.

'Yes. And they want the reward to go to Rodger's staff. The thing is the painting is hideous. The most revolting thing I've ever seen. The whole village came out to look at it. They had such a laugh. You really missed something this morning,' he said.

'Trust me to go away when something interesting happens,' I said. 'Is the painting truly vile?'

'Utterly, utterly disgusting. If Rodger Barnes paid thirty thousand for that he's a bigger mug than I thought he was. And I've always thought he was an idiot. He's got a really red face now.'

'Ha. Ha,' I said.

'I doubt the insurance company will stump up when they see the picture. Any fool can see it's worthless. Besides they won't have to pay up. The picture's back. But they'll be having a look at the rest of his collection,' said Dad.

'Excellent,' I said. Nice one, I thought.

After I'd rung off, I told Tina. We spent half an hour jumping about waving our fists in the air. We'd done it. At last, after my protest all those years ago, I'd finally struck a blow for battery chickens.

Who knows, I thought, he might even be investigated by the police. Maybe he'd be suspected of insurance fraud. Maybe he'd be discovered to be paying low wages. Maybe he'd be closed down. All in all, I decided, it was an excellent result.

WHO IS WATCHING WHO?

I started my new job. I loved it. The restaurant was called EO's. Meaning Everything Organic. The people I worked with were wonderful. And the customers were fun, and liked the food I cooked.

You could say I was happy. I loved Glasgow. It's a humming place. Great nightlife, friendly folk. After years in a village, my life was a whirl. I made new friends. I was on top of the world.

Then, I started to notice things. I walked to work every day. I passed beggars. I saw a lot of lonely people. I saw sad faces. It's the same everywhere. It came to me that if the Cherry Sundae Company could make a difference in a small village, it could do a lot for a big city.

I asked Tim and Jane, my employers, if I could put a charity box on the bar at the restaurant.

'You know,' I said. 'I could collect money for AIDS or Save The Whale. Oh, all sorts of things. People could just drop a few coins in as they are paying their bills.'

Tim and Jane agreed. Glaswegians are generous. Soon I had money to drop in beggars' boxes, and I bought the Big Issue regularly from various vendors. I donated money to the homeless. I bought a new coat for an old man who looked cold.

It's just the way things are, these days. People make a bad decision and find themselves out of work. Then they can't pay their rent, and get kicked out of their homes.

It seems to me that sometimes people take the wrong path in life, they choose the difficult road and everything turns out bad for them. I always think it could happen to me. I always think I should do something.

Last week I dropped an envelope through the letter box of an old couple across the road from me. I'd seen them come and go. You don't need brains to see they are struggling. I'd heard someone in the street mention they were cold because they couldn't afford to put their heating on.

Greetings from the Cherry Sundae Company, my note said. We have noticed how you smile to your neighbours. In the summer your window boxes are beautiful. Here's a reward for the pleasure you bring.

I'd slipped five twenty pound notes, cash from the collection box at the restaurant and changed at the bank, into the envelope along with my note.

Remember, my letter ended, your good deeds will be returned to you many times.

I saw the old couple a few days later. I thought they were walking in a more upright way, less stooped.

They looked warmer.

Yesterday morning, I got up at seven. I showered and put on the kettle to make coffee before going to work. I heard the post rattle through the letter box, and went into the hall to pick it up. I wasn't feeling all that happy. Mostly I get bills.

But there was a letter for me. It had my name and address on the front. I turned it over in my hands wondering who it could be from.

The envelope was dark blue, it felt expensive. My name was in red ink. I ripped open the seal. The letter inside was also written on blue paper. The heading was The Knickerbocker Glory Company. The what? I thought.

I read.

Greetings from the Raspberry Surprise Company. We know all about you. We are looking out for you. Remember your good deeds, and your naughty deeds will be returned to you many times.

It wasn't signed. Who could have sent it? I didn't know. But I had the creepy feeling that someone was watching me.

I walked to work looking about me, trying to spot someone who might be observing me from afar. Every now and then I whirled round, checking that I wasn't being followed.

The Raspberry Surprise Company knows all about me. My naughty deeds will be returned to me many times. Oh goodness me.

Of course, it said my good deeds will be returned to me too. But it's the naughty ones I'm worried about.

The Cherry Sundae Company cut down a man's hedge without permission. It brought havoc into a battery chicken farm. It made a laughing stock of a man's art collection and cost him fifteen thousand pounds.

I have to take care. I have to watch

out. There are people out there who are bound to be seeking revenge.

This item must be returned or renewed on or before the latest date shown

Miss Parr. 2	3	